Merry Bay – Engine Failure

Nikki Payne

Merry Bay – Engine Failure

Olympia Publishers
London

www.olympiapublishers.com
OLYMPIA PAPERBACK EDITION

A CIP catalogue record for this title is available from the British Library.

ISBN: 978-1-78830-600-3

First Published in 2020

Olympia Publishers
Tallis House
2 Tallis Street
London
EC4Y 0AB

Printed in Great Britain

Dedication

Merry Bay - Engine Failure is dedicated to Fred and Dylis Creech.

Acknowledgements

Once again acknowledgement goes to my amazing husband, Marcus, for his continued support and encouragement.

It had been quiet in Merry Bay for the last week, but today was Saturday, the sun was shining and the town was bustling with people. Fred the all-weather lifeboat, was bobbing on his pontoon and smiling at the visitors who were taking pictures of him as they walked by.

"I'm glad I've already had my bath." He thought.

"Smile, Fred," called Mrs Crump as she positioned her two children on the pontoon in front of him for a photograph.

Jim, the Coxswain, was watching from inside the lifeboat station. He smiled as he watched Fred give Mrs Crump his biggest grin.

Charlie the seagull wandered into the lifeboat station carrying a cone of chips.

"Hello, Jim," He squawked.

"Hello, Charlie. Where did you get those?" Jim replied. "I hope you didn't pinch them from someone."

"No," said Charlie. "I found them in the Quay fish and chip shop. They had been left on the counter!"

Jim laughed, "CHARLIE."

Charlie flapped his wings and swallowed hard. "Hmm, they were nice," He said with a smile.

"Hello, Jim," said Mrs Crump as she walked towards the lifeboat station. "How are you?"

"Very well, thank you, Mrs Crump. How are you and the twins?"

Mrs Crump and Jim both looked across at the two girls who were now laughing and chasing Charlie up and down the slipway.

"I can't wear them out," she said shaking her head. "I'm taking them to see Mr Fisk. He is going to take them fishing for the afternoon."

"THAT'S ENOUGH," squawked Charlie. Jim and Mrs Crump both turned to find Charlie panting on the slipway in front of the two giggling twins

"Huh, huh, huh," He panted.

"That's all those chips, Charlie," called Fred. "They are weighing you down."

Everyone laughed.

Mrs Crump and the twins said their goodbyes and carried on their way to find Mr Fisk. Jim returned to the lifeboat station where he picked up a broom from its resting place on the side wall and started to sweep away the crumbs from Charlie's chips.

Although there were lots of people in Merry Bay today, the afternoon passed by uneventfully. Jim was sat in the back room drinking a cup of tea when Sally arrived for her shift.

"Hello, Fred," she called as she passed the all-weather lifeboat pontoon. "Anything happening today?"

"No," said Fred. "Except the Crump twins came by. They chased Charlie around the slipway. It was very funny."

Sally laughed, "Oh dear."

Ping! Ping! Ping!

PING, PING, PING, the computer in the back room noisily sprung into life.

"Just in time," said Sally, as she ran into the lifeboat station. Jim was already reading the message on the screen when Sally reached the back room.

FISHING BOAT ENGINE FAILURE. FIVE MILES OFF BLACKSAND HEAD. THREE PERSONS ON BOARD.

"Hmmm," said Jim. "I think we will need Fred for this one, Sally. I'm not sure Susie or Derek will be strong enough to tow the fishing boat back to Merry Quay. It's quite a long way!"

"I think you are right, Jim," Sally replied. She turned and hit the big red button on the wall which had the words 'ANNIE' written on it.

WOOO LIFEBOAT LAUNCHING, WOOO LIFEBOAT LAUNCHING, WOOO LIFEBOAT LAUNCHING, WOOO LIFEBOAT LAUNCHING, WOOO LIFEBOAT LAUNCHING.

"Keep watch, Susie," called Jim as he and Sally grabbed their helmets and life jackets from the wall, and ran out of the lifeboat station towards the all-weather lifeboat pontoon.

"Blacksand Head, Fred," called Jim as Sally set about untying Fred's mooring ropes. "Quick as you can." And with that, Fred left the pontoon and was heading across the bay in the direction of Blacksand Head.

Although it was a sunny day, the sea was very choppy and Fred bobbed from side to side as he raced across the water.

"Woooo lifeboat launching!!"
"Woooo lifeboat launching!!"
"Woooo lifeboat launching!!"

"Hellllooo," came a soft voice from the water. Sally looked over Fred's port side where the voice had come from. Dylis the Dolphin and her pup, Rhys, were swimming in the water.

"Hi, Dylis," called Sally. "We are on a shout. Have you seen a fishing boat in difficulty about five miles off Blacksand Head?" She asked.

"I have," Dylis replied. She was now standing up out of the water splashing her tail to keep herself upright. "It is Mr Fisk and the Crump twins. Rhys was playing just off the muscle farm nearby when Mr Fisk called across to say that his engine had failed and could he keep an eye out for you."

"OK Dylis," shouted Fred above the noise of his engine. "You lead the way."

Dylis and Rhys swam ahead of Fred's hull until they reached Mr Fisk's position off Blacksand Head.

The boat was a large blue wooden boat with a wide deck and a small enclosed forward cabin. As Fred neared the location, Sally spotted the boat and called to Jim.

"I can see them, Jim. Over there." Sally pointed with both hands towards the stranded vessel as Fred turned and headed over to where Mr Fisk and the Crump twins were waiting for them.

"Hello there," called Mr Fisk as Fred pulled alongside.

"Hello," Jim replied. "Is everyone ok?"

"We are," said Mr Fisk. "Although one of the twins is feeling a little sea sick with all this bobbing about."

"Glad to see you all wearing life jackets," Sally shouted across. "You would be surprised how many times we get called out to boats where there are no life jackets on board."

"Always make sure I wear one," said Mr Fisk. "It would be foolish not to."

"Quite right," Replied Jim.

"I think it would be better if we get the girls on board, Fred," said Jim. "Are you ok to stay on your boat and we will tow you back?"

"Sure thing, Jim."

"Steady, Fred, this is going to be tricky. Sally, can you throw a rope over to Mr Fisk?"

Sally threw the mooring line across to Mr Fisk, which he tied around his starboard cleat. Jim looked at the two rather green Crump twins standing on the deck. "One at a time; Mr Fisk will lift you up and pass you over here."

"Steady now, Fred," he said as Mr Fisk lifted the first twin over the side of the fishing boat and onto the deck of the all-weather lifeboat. Once both girls were safely on-board, Sally handed one of the twin's a bag as she was still feeling very queasy!

Jim threw Mr Fisk a long thick rope which he tied to the front of the fishing boat. "Let's get you back to shore," he called. Mr Fisk waved to Dylis and Rhys who were still watching from the water. "Thank you both," he called.

Bleep... Bloop... Bleep... Bloop... Bleep... Bloop...

As Fred sped across the bay, Jim spoke into the VHF radio he was wearing on his life jacket. "Merry Bay Coastguard, Merry Bay Coastguard, this is all-weather lifeboat, over."

"All-weather lifeboat this is Merry Bay Coastguard over," came the reply.

"We have the boat secured and are heading for Merry Quay. There are no injuries on board. Can you please ring Mrs Crump and ask her to come and pick up the twins. One is feeling sea sick."

"Thank you, all-weather lifeboat. We will arrange for Mrs Crump to meet you there. Merry Bay Coastguard out."

After Fred had dropped Mr Fisk, his fishing boat and the Crump twins off at Merry Quay, he raced back towards Merry Bay. He wasn't smiling now. In fact, Fred looked very glum.

"Oh my," said Susie, as Fred moored up on his pontoon. "Whatever is wrong?" she asked worriedly.

Jim and Sally roared with laughter as they climbed down from Fred's deck onto the pontoon. From inside the lifeboat station, Susie could see a large light brown coloured patch on Fred's foredeck.

"Is that what I think it is?" Susie asked. Jim and Sally nodded.

"Yes," said Fred miserably. "The bag split!"

"Ha ha ha ha ha," all laughed.